A Monster House

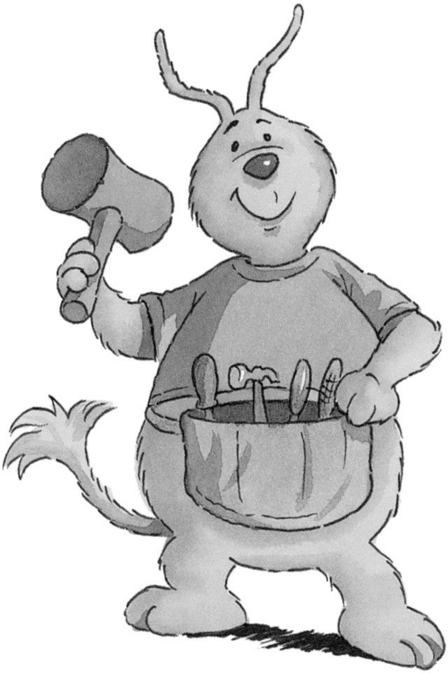

Illustrated by Richard Hoit

Rigby

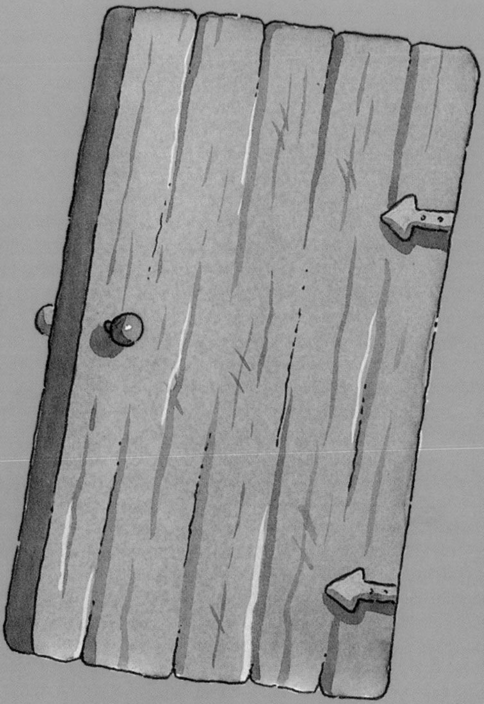

a door

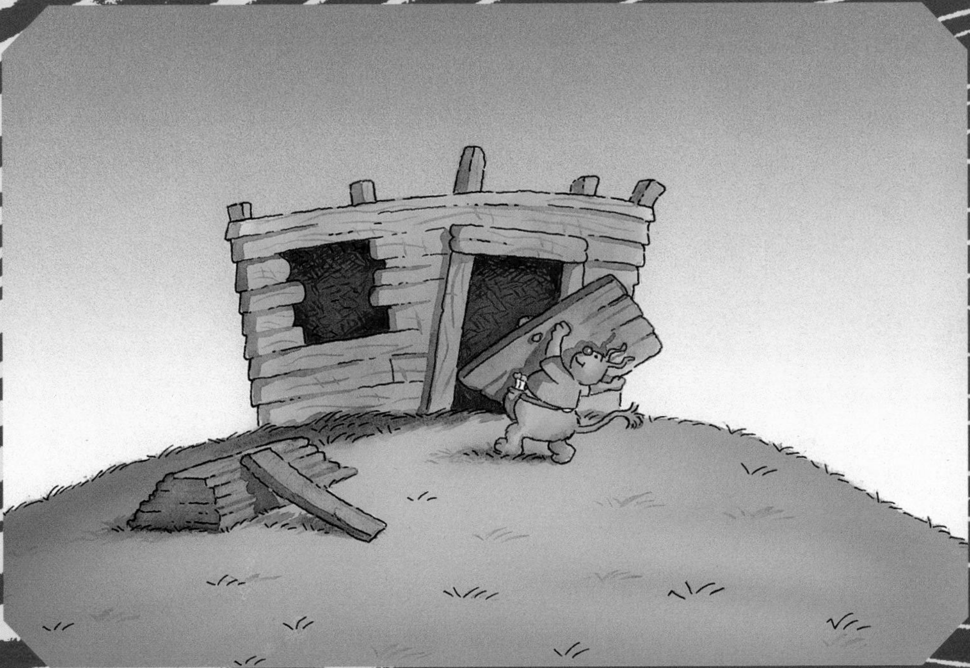

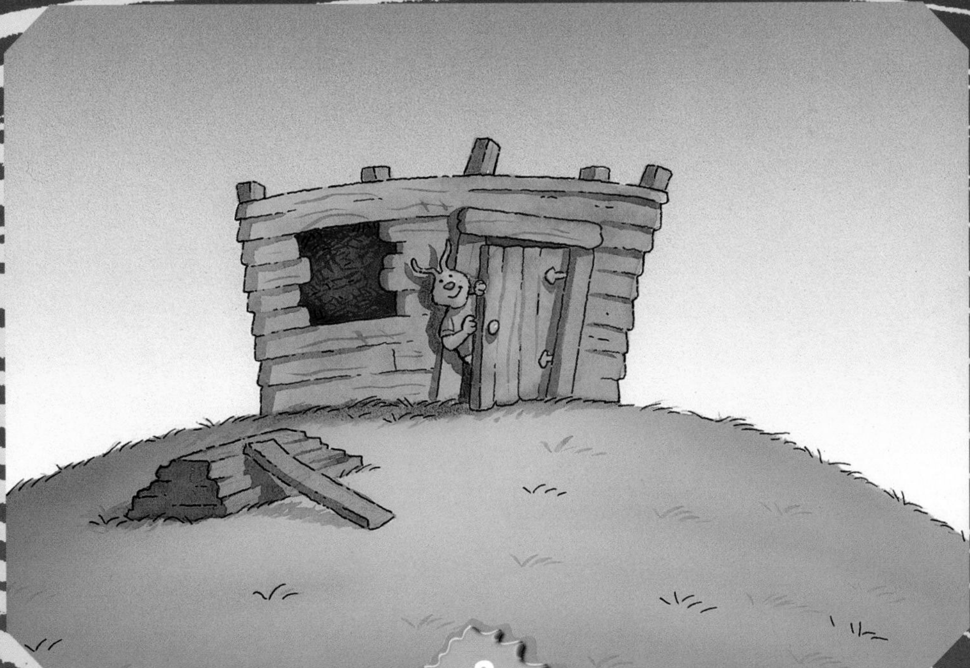

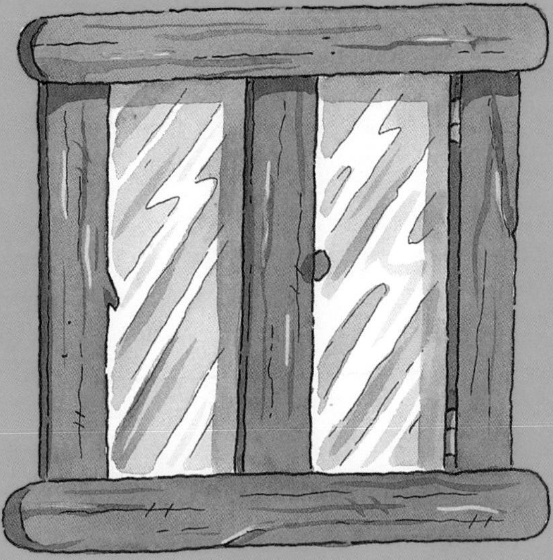

a window

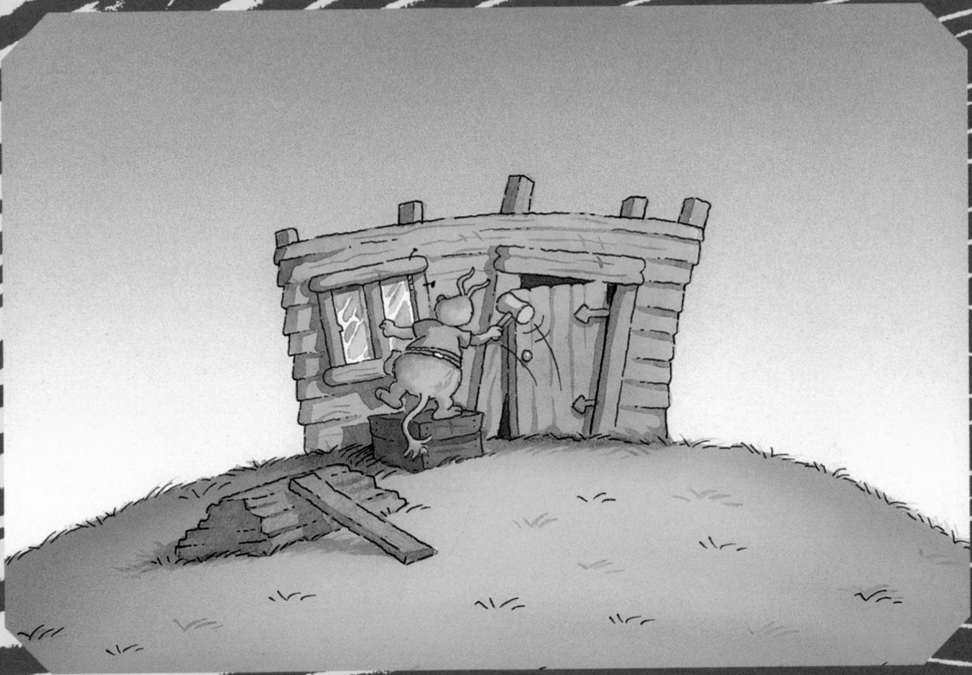

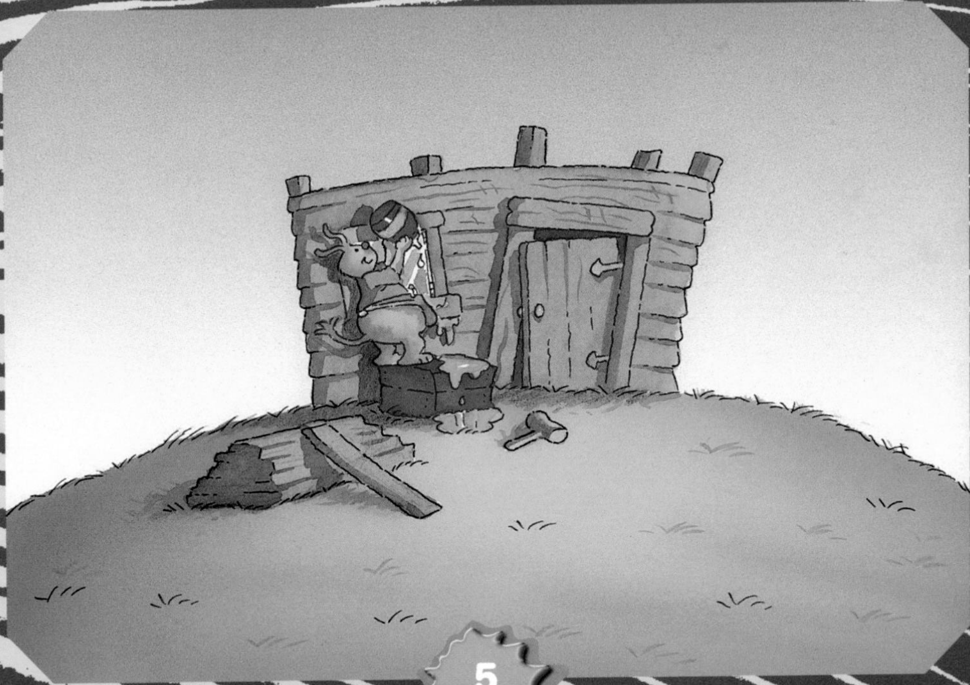

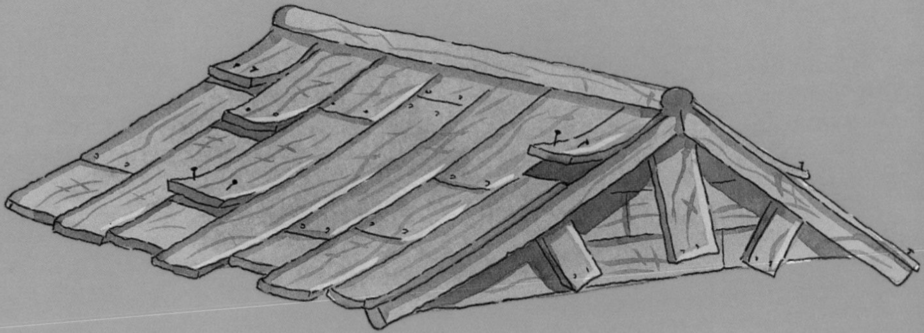

a roof

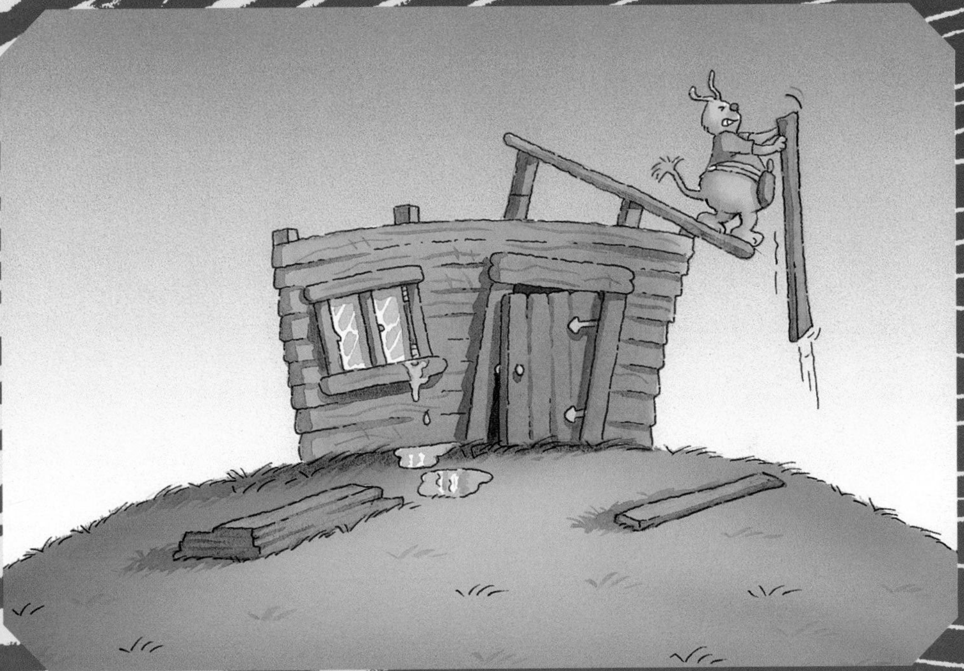

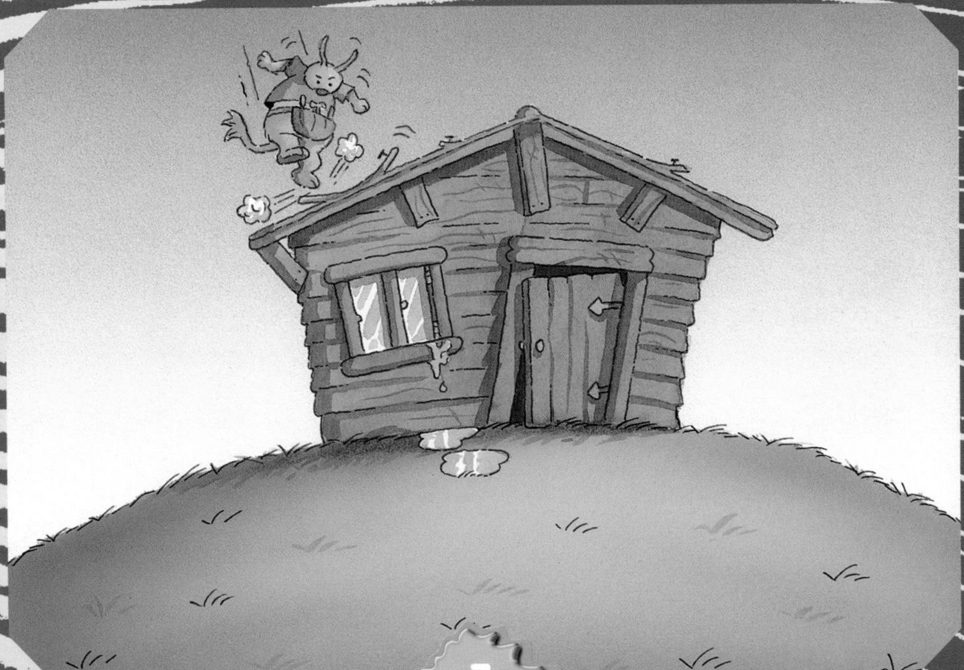

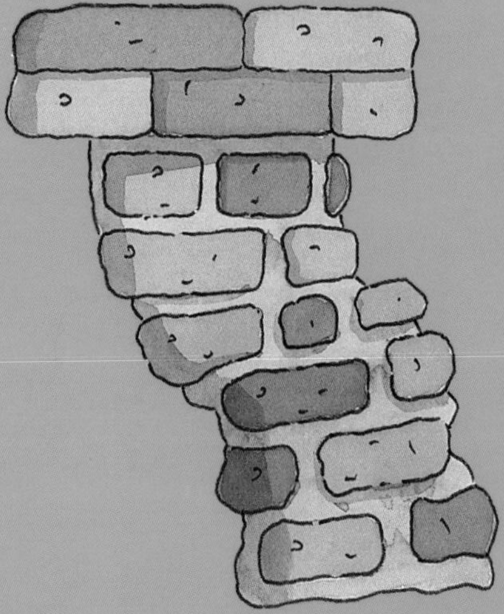

a chimney

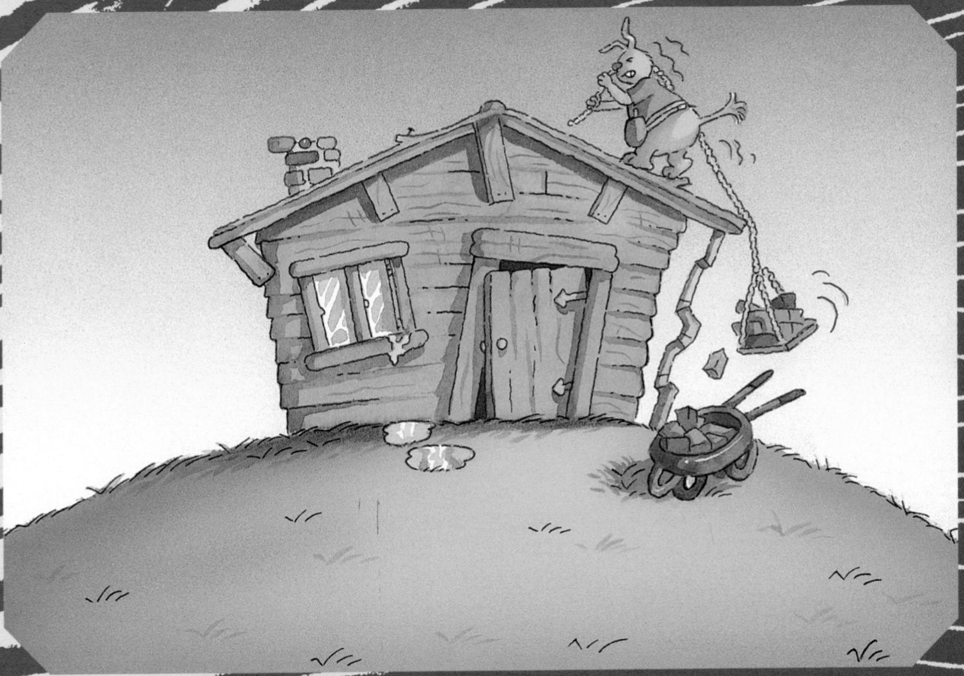

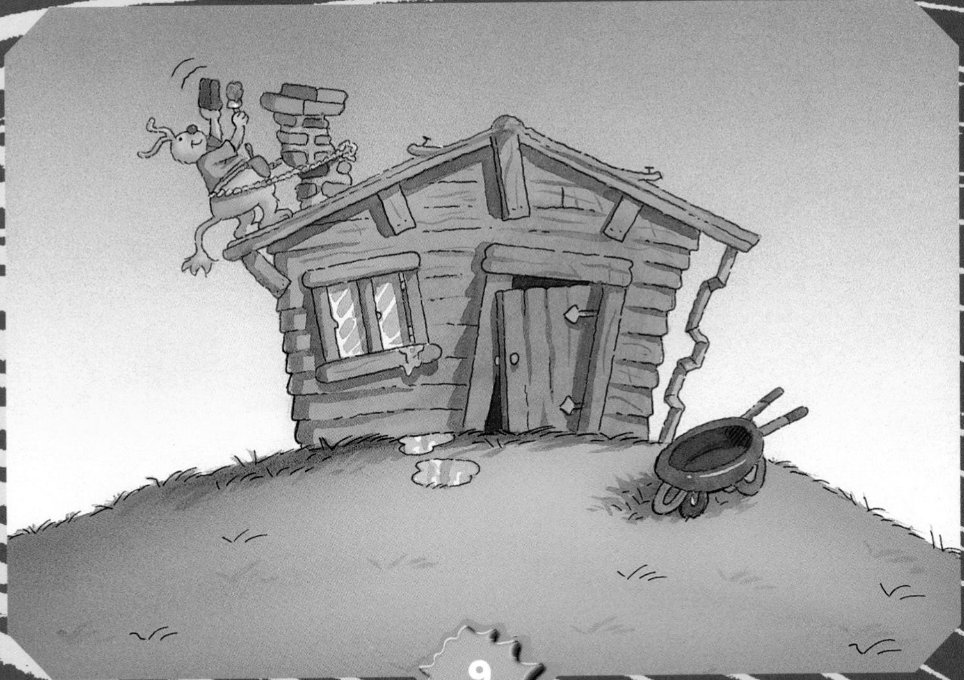

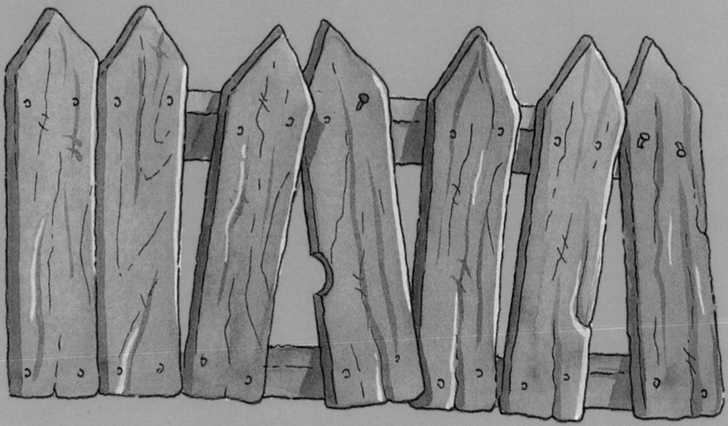

a fence

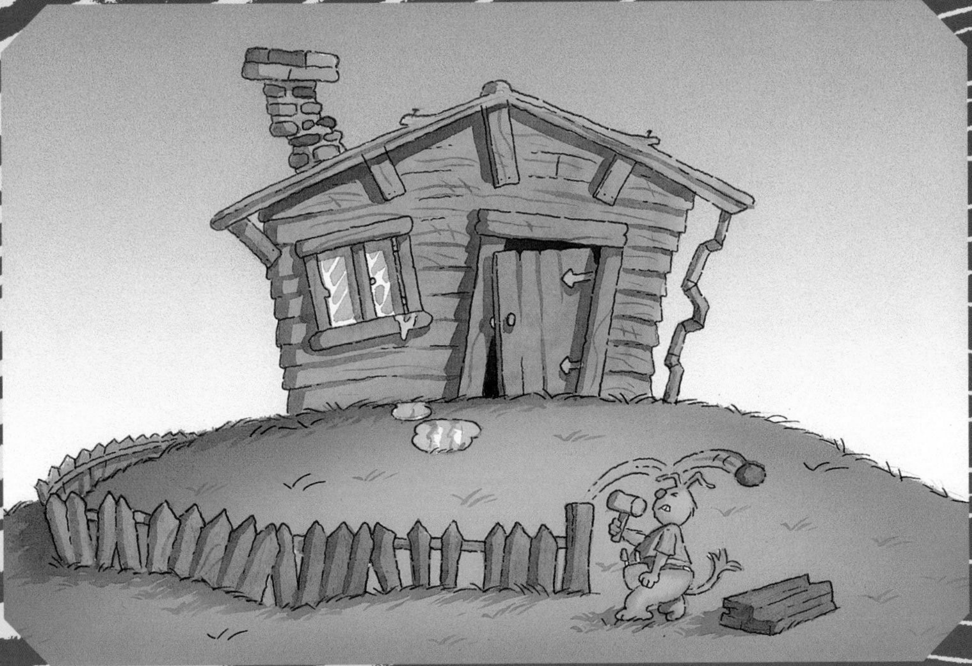

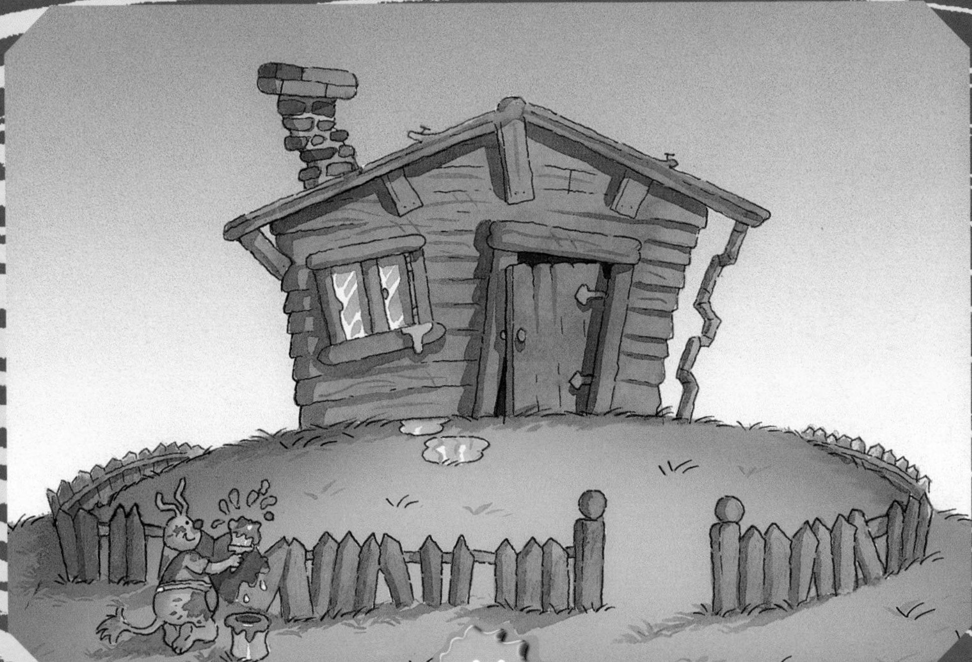

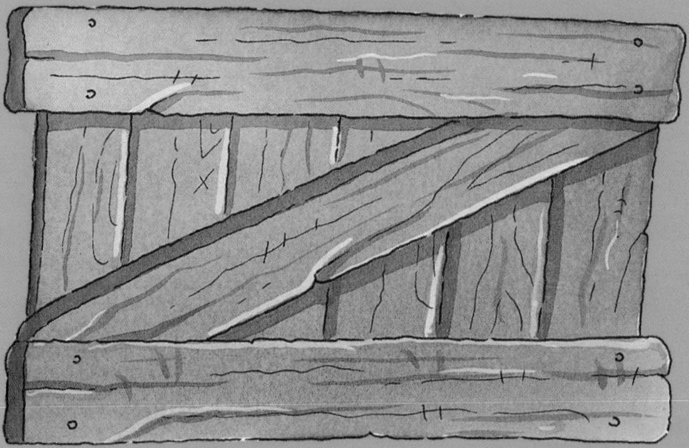

a gate

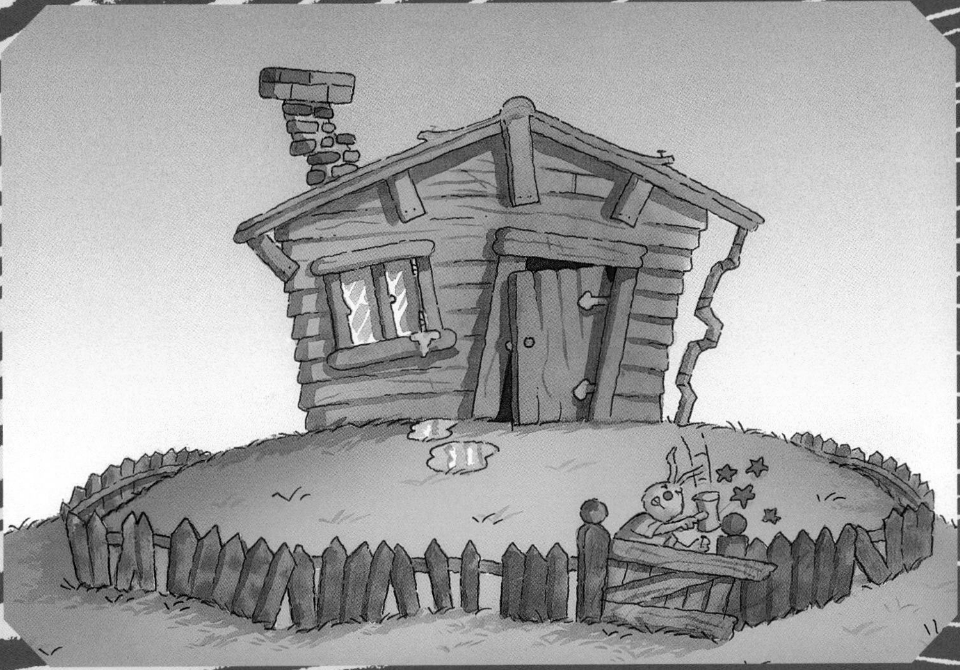

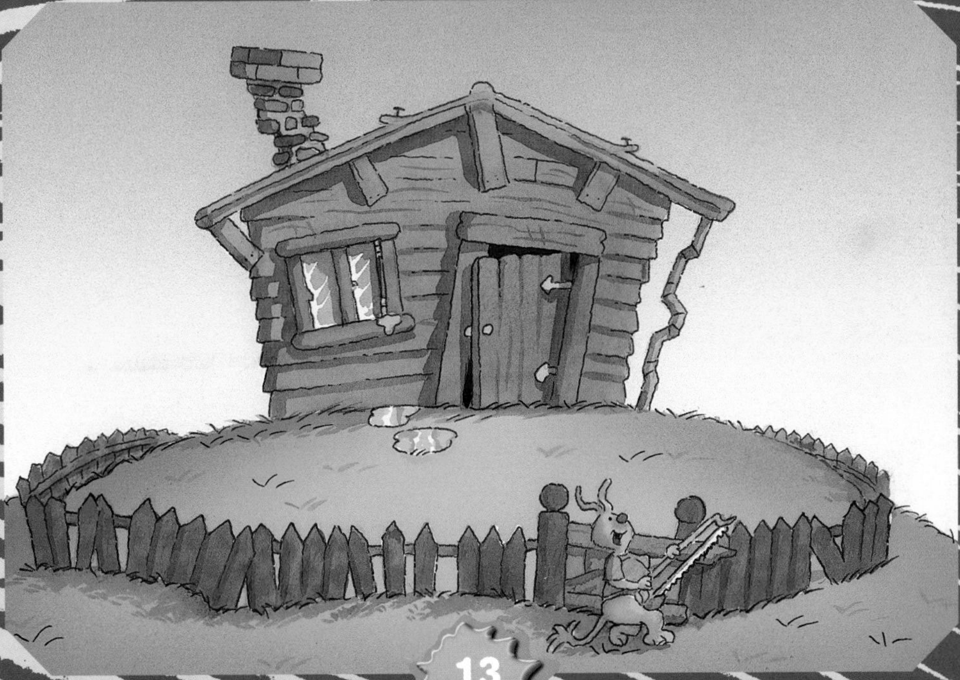

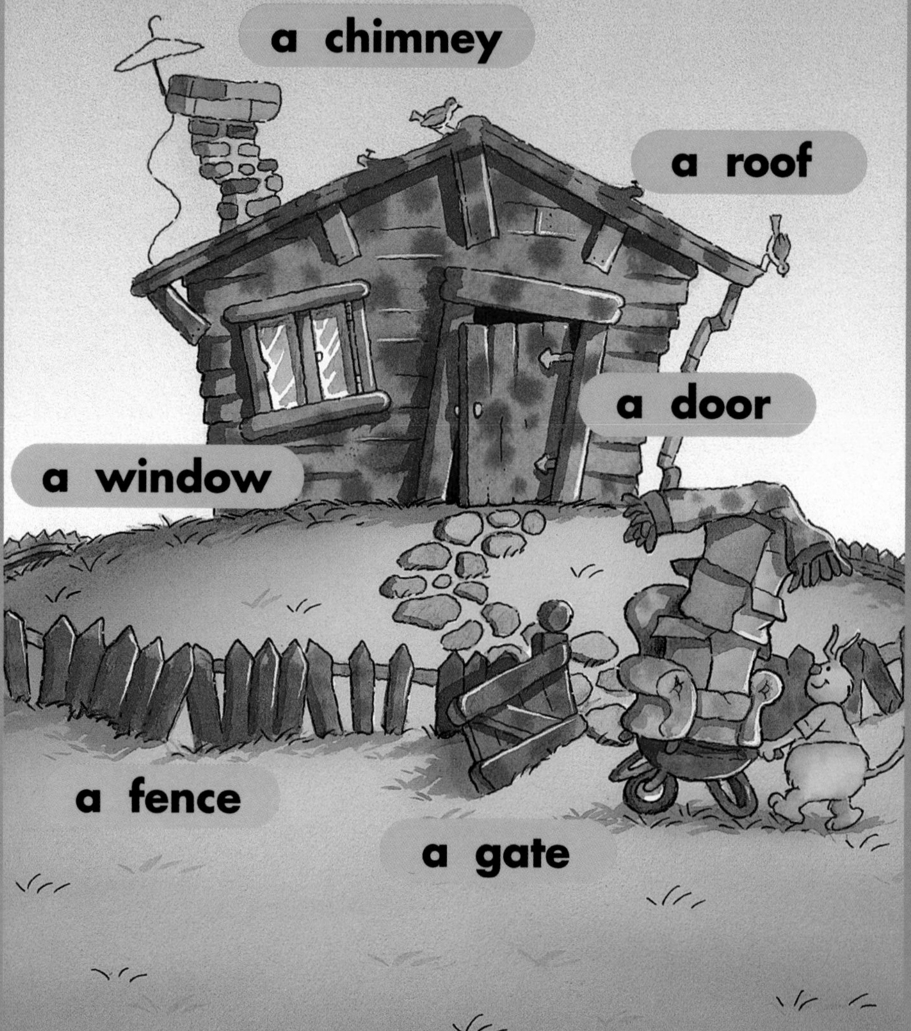
a chimney
a roof
a door
a window
a fence
a gate

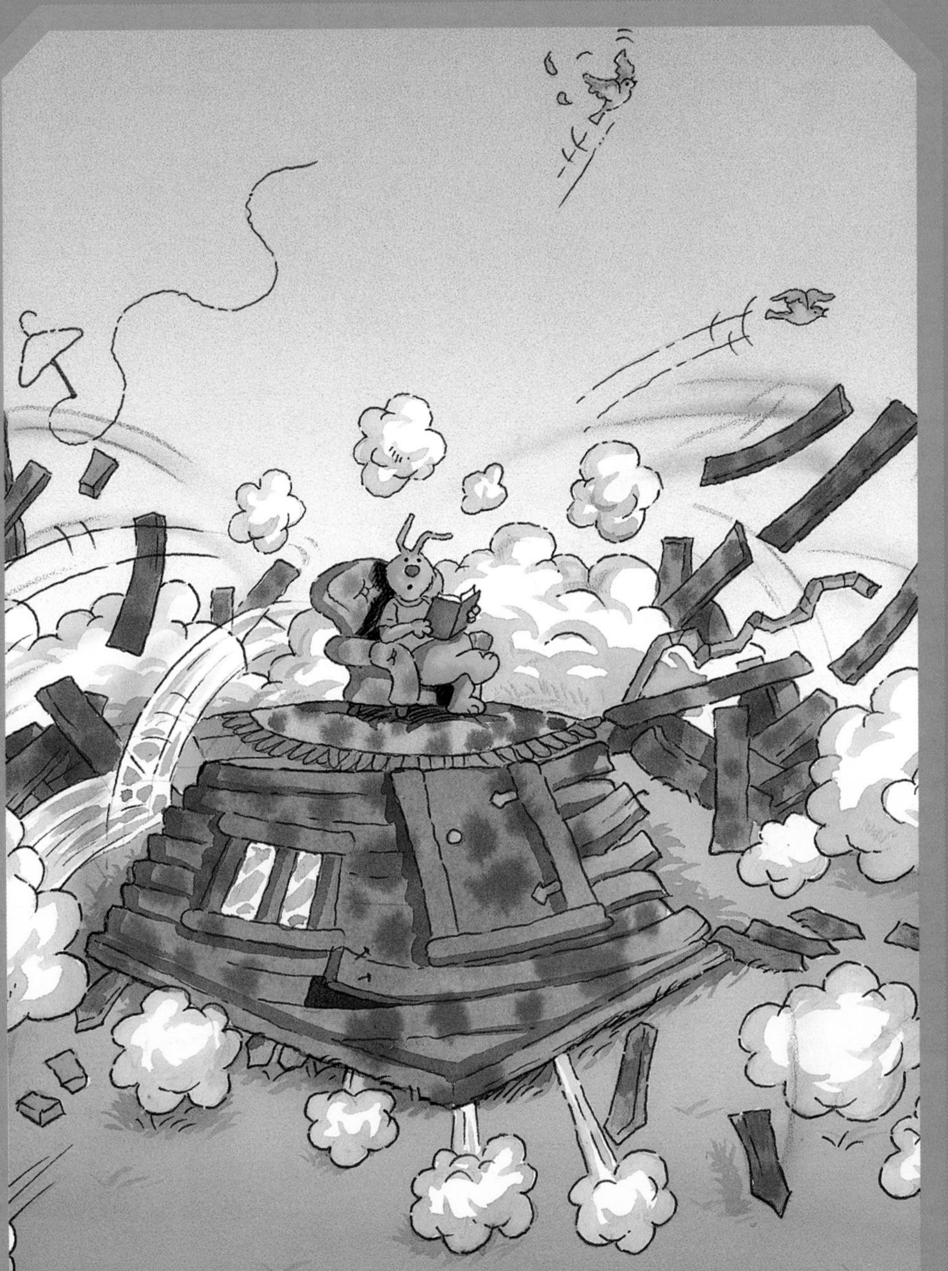

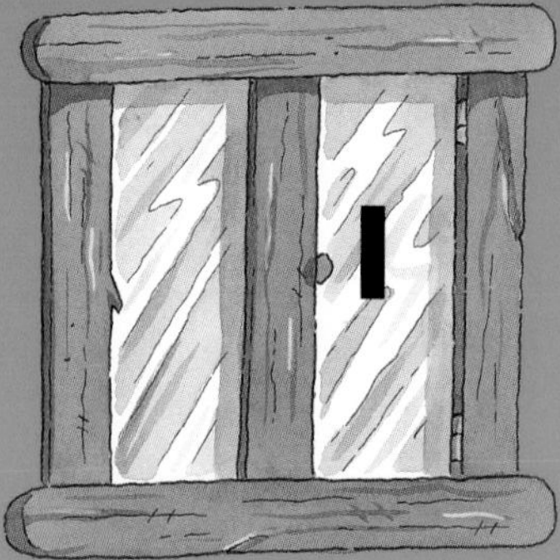
I
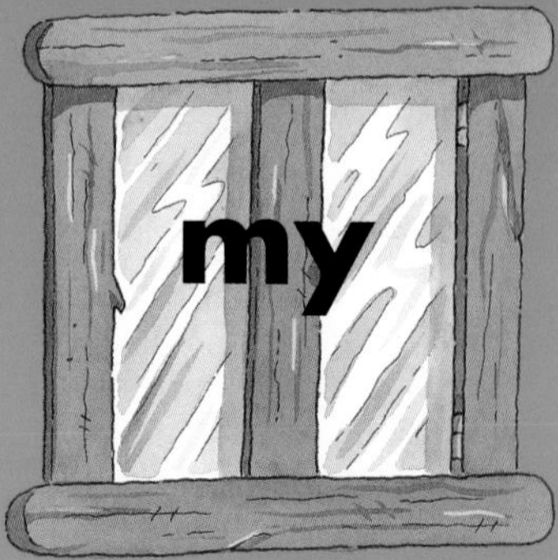
my
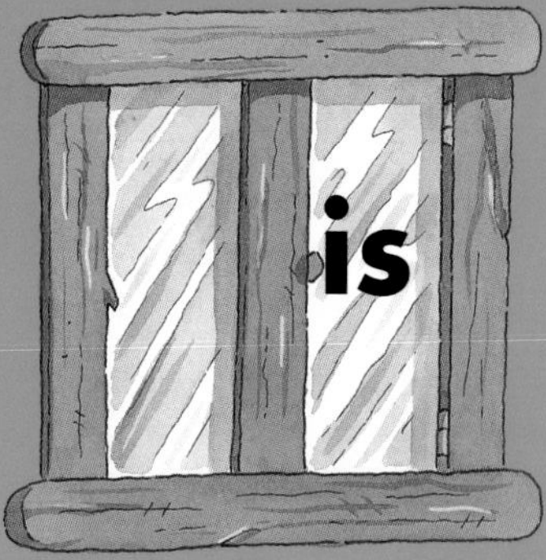
is
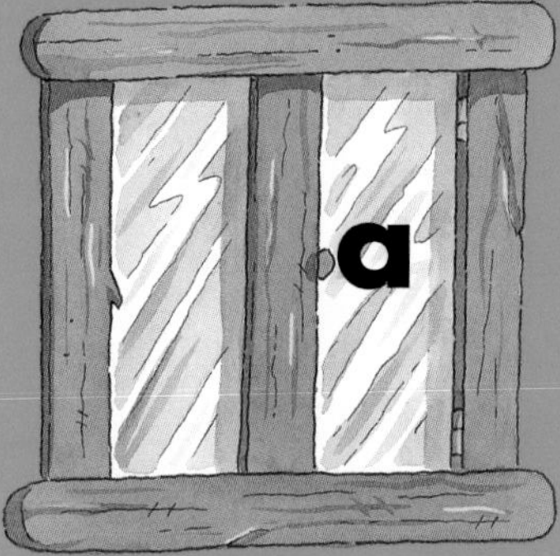
a
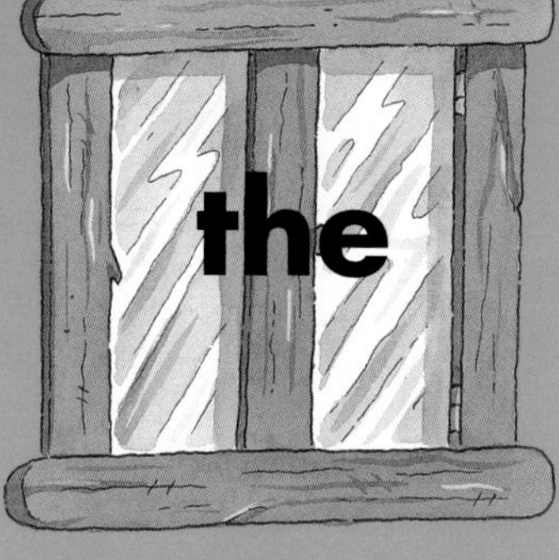
the
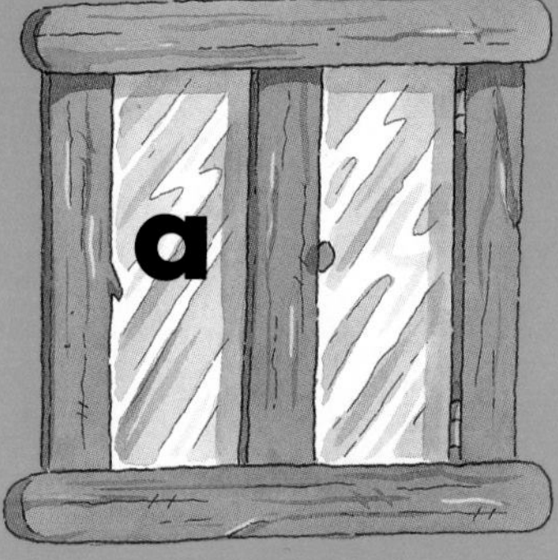
a